SO-AYZ-206

THE TALE

OF

MRS. TIGGY-WINKLE

THE TALE OF
MRS. TIGGY-WINKLE

BY

BEATRIX POTTER

Author of
"The Tale of Peter Rabbit," &c.

DOVER PUBLICATIONS, INC.
NEW YORK

This Dover edition, first published in 1973, is an unabridged republication of the work first published in 1905.

International Standard Book Number: 0-486-20546-0
Library of Congress Catalog Card Number: 73-84197

Manufactured in the United States of America
Dover Publications, Inc.
180 Varick Street
New York, N. Y. 10014

For

THE REAL LITTLE LUCIE

OF NEWLANDS.

ONCE upon a time there was a little girl called Lucie, who lived at a farm called Little-town. She was a good little girl—only she was always losing her pocket-handkerchiefs!

One day little Lucie came into the farm-yard crying— oh, she did cry so! "I've lost my pocket-handkin! Three handkins and a pinny! Have *you* seen them, Tabby Kitten?"

THE Kitten went on washing her white paws; so Lucie asked a speckled hen—

"Sally Henny-penny, have *you* found three pocket-handkins?"

But the speckled hen ran into a barn, clucking—

"I go barefoot, barefoot, barefoot!"

AND then Lucie asked Cock Robin sitting on a twig.

Cock Robin looked sideways at Lucie with his bright black eye, and he flew over a stile and away.

Lucie climbed upon the stile and looked up at the hill behind Little-town—a hill that goes up — up — into the clouds as though it had no top!

And a great way up the hillside she thought she saw some white things spread upon the grass.

LUCIE scrambled up the hill as fast as her short legs would carry her; she ran along a steep path-way—up and up—until Little-town was right away down below—she could have dropped a pebble down the chimney!

PRESENTLY she came to a spring, bubbling out from the hill side.

Some one had stood a tin can upon a stone to catch the water — but the water was already running over, for the can was no bigger than an egg-cup! And where the sand upon the path was wet—there were foot-marks of a *very* small person.

Lucie ran on, and on.

THE path ended under a big rock. The grass was short and green, and there were clothes-props cut from bracken stems, with lines of plaited rushes, and a heap of tiny clothes pins—but no pocket-handkerchiefs!

But there was something else—a door! straight into the hill; and inside it some one was singing—

"Lily-white and clean, oh!
With little frills between, oh!
Smooth and hot—red rusty spot
Never here be seen, oh!"

LUCIE knocked—once—
twice, and interrupted
the song. A little frightened
voice called out "Who's that?"

Lucie opened the door: and
what do you think there was
inside the hill?—a nice clean
kitchen with a flagged floor
and wooden beams—just like
any other farm kitchen. Only
the ceiling was so low that
Lucie's head nearly touched it;
and the pots and pans were
small, and so was everything
there.

THERE was a nice hot singey smell; and at the table, with an iron in her hand, stood a very stout short person staring anxiously at Lucie.

Her print gown was tucked up, and she was wearing a large apron over her striped petticoat. Her little black nose went sniffle, sniffle, snuffle, and her eyes went twinkle, twinkle; and underneath her cap—where Lucie had yellow curls—that little person had PRICKLES!

"WHO are you?" said
Lucie. "Have you
seen my pocket-handkins?"

The little person made a
bob-curtsey—"Oh yes, if you
please'm; my name is Mrs.
Tiggy-winkle; oh yes if you
please'm, I'm an excellent clear-
starcher!" And she took
something out of a clothes-
basket, and spread it on the
ironing-blanket.

"WHAT'S that thing?"
said Lucie — "that's
not my pocket-handkin?"

"Oh no, if you please'm;
that's a little scarlet waist-coat
belonging to Cock Robin!"

And she ironed it and folded
it, and put it on one side.

THEN she took something else off a clothes-horse—

"That isn't my pinny?" said Lucie.

"Oh no, if you please'm; that's a damask table-cloth belonging to Jenny Wren; look how it's stained with currant wine! It's very bad to wash!" said Mrs. Tiggy-winkle.

MRS. TIGGY-WINKLE'S
nose went sniffle sniffle
snuffle, and her eyes went
twinkle twinkle; and she
fetched another hot iron from
the fire.

"THERE'S one of my pocket-handkins!" cried Lucie—"and there's my pinny!"

Mrs. Tiggy-winkle ironed it, and goffered it, and shook out the frills.

"Oh that *is* lovely!" said Lucie.

"AND what are those long yellow things with fingers like gloves?"

"Oh that's a pair of stockings belonging to Sally Henny-penny—look how she's worn the heels out with scratching in the yard! She'll very soon go barefoot!" said Mrs. Tiggy-winkle.

"WHY, there's another handkersniff — but it isn't mine; it's red?"

"Oh no, if you please'm; that one belongs to old Mrs. Rabbit; and it *did* so smell of onions! I've had to wash it separately, I can't get out the smell."

"There's another one of mine, said Lucie.

"WHAT are those funny little white things?"

"That's a pair of mittens belonging to Tabby Kitten; I only have to iron them; she washes them herself."

"There's my last pocket-handkin!" said Lucie.

"AND what are you dipping into the basin of starch?"

"They're little dicky shirt-fronts belonging to Tom Tit-mouse—most terrible particular!" said Mrs. Tiggy-winkle. "Now I've finished my ironing; I'm going to air some clothes."

"WHAT are these dear soft fluffy things?" said Lucie.

"Oh those are woolly coats belonging to the little lambs at Skelghyl."

"Will their jackets take off?" asked Lucie.

"Oh yes, if you please'm; look at the sheep-mark on the shoulder. And here's one marked for Gatesgarth, and three that come from Little-town. They're *always* marked at washing!" said Mrs. Tiggy-winkle.

AND she hung up all sorts and sizes of clothes— small brown coats of mice; and one velvety black mole-skin waist-coat; and a red tail-coat with no tail belonging to Squirrel Nutkin; and a very much shrunk blue jacket belonging to Peter Rabbit; and a petticoat, not marked, that had gone lost in the washing —and at last the basket was empty!

THEN Mrs. Tiggy-winkle made tea—a cup for herself and a cup for Lucie. They sat before the fire on a bench and looked sideways at one another. Mrs. Tiggy-winkle's hand, holding the tea-cup, was very very brown, and very very wrinkly with the soap-suds; and all through her gown and her cap, there were *hair-pins* sticking wrong end out; so that Lucie didn't like to sit too near her.

WHEN they had finished tea, they tied up the clothes in bundles; and Lucie's pocket-handkerchiefs were folded up inside her clean pinny, and fastened with a silver safety-pin.

And then they made up the fire with turf, and came out and locked the door, and hid the key under the door-sill.

THEN away down the hill trotted Lucie and Mrs. Tiggy-winkle with the bundles of clothes!

All the way down the path little animals came out of the fern to meet them; the very first that they met were Peter Rabbit and Benjamin Bunny!

AND she gave them their nice clean clothes; and all the little animals and birds were so very much obliged to dear Mrs. Tiggy-winkle.

SO that at the bottom of the hill when they came to the stile, there was nothing left to carry except Lucie's one little bundle.

LUCIE scrambled up the stile with the bundle in her hand; and then she turned to say "Good-night," and to thank the washer-woman.— But what a *very* odd thing! Mrs. Tiggy-winkle had not waited either for thanks or for the washing bill!

She was running running running up the hill — and where was her white frilled cap? and her shawl? and her gown—and her petticoat?

A<small>ND</small> *how* small she had grown—and *how* brown —and covered with P<small>RICKLES</small>! Why! Mrs. Tiggy-winkle was nothing but a H<small>EDGEHOG</small>!

*   *   *   *   *   *

(Now some people say that little Lucie had been asleep upon the stile— but then how could she have found three clean pocket-handkins and a pinny, pinned with a silver safety-pin?

And besides—*I* have seen that door into the back of the hill called Cat Bells — and besides *I* am very well acquainted with dear Mrs. Tiggy-winkle!)

T<small>HE</small> E<small>ND</small>.